聪明的伙伴
The clever friends

疼呀痛啊

Ache and Pain

肖叶文

罗殷 焦天虹图

[美]斯蒂芬妮·陈译

连环画出版社
北京

一场鹅毛大雪下过以后，小动物们都跑到外面玩起了打雪仗。忽然，一个雪球打在狐狸小皮的脑袋上，她喊道："哎哟，好疼啊！"

After a heavy snowstorm, all the friends went outside
to have a snowball fight. A snowball hit Xiaopi in the
head and she exclaimed, "Ahhh! It hurts!"

这时，胖熊点点也被一个大大的雪球去中了，雪顺着他的脖子往里钻。

Around the same time, Diandian also got hit by a huge snowball. Snow trickled down his neck.

胖熊点点大声叫道："我的妈呀，真是**透心凉**啊！"

Diandian yelled, "It's **freezing**!"

胖熊点点和狐狸小皮一起来到雪人的身边。狐狸小皮亲了亲雪人，说道："可爱的雪人，你的脸这么凉，难道你不怕冷吗？"

Diandian and Xiaopi came to a snowman. Xiaopi kissed the snowman and said, "Your face feels cold. Aren't you afraid of coldness?"

"驾！快跑！"胖熊点点开心地骑上了冰雕的小马，得意地喊道，"哇！又凉又硬，硌屁股呀！"

"Giddy-up!" Diandian excitedly rode on a horse made out of ice and shouted, "Ahhh! This horse is so hard and cold. It hurts my butt!"

熊妈妈推开家门，对小动物们喊道："孩子们，外面太冷了，快进屋暖和暖和吧！"

Mama Bear opened the door and shouted,
"Kids, it's so cold outside. Why don't you all
come in and warm up a little bit."

胖熊点点一边烤火一边说："哇，好暖和呀！"
熊妈妈递给狐狸小皮一杯热牛奶。"谢谢！"狐狸
小皮说，"哎呀！太烫啦！我得晾凉了再喝。"

Diandian warmed up by the fireplace and said, "Wow!
It's so warm!" Mama Bear handed Xiaopi a glass of hot
milk. "Thank you!" said Xiaopi, "Oh! It's too hot! I have
to let it cool down before I drink."

这时候，胖熊点点对大家说："咱们来玩抱抱游戏吧！"

At this time, Diandian said to everyone, "Let's play the hugging game!"

小猫忙说："那我把你的眼睛蒙上，你来猜一猜吧！"

Little Cat said, "Okay. I'll cover your eyes, and you guess first!"

"尖尖的嘴，软软的羽毛，细长
的腿……"胖熊点点一边摸一边猜，
"是大公鸡吗？"

大公鸡说："对啦，对啦！"

"Sharp beak, soft feather, long and
skinny legs..." Diandian continued to
guess, "Is it Big Rooster?"
Big Rooster said, "You got it!"

"小小的耳朵，翘翘的鼻子，热乎乎的嘴……"
胖熊点点猜道，"是河马吗？"
河马说："哇！你太厉害了！是我，是我！"

"Small ears, upturned nose, warm mouth…" Diandian guess, "Is it Hippo?"
Hippo said, "Wow, you're good at this! It's me. It's me!"

"长长的耳朵，圆圆的脸，毛茸茸的身子，还有短短的尾巴……"胖熊点点猜道，"是小兔子吗？"

小兔子说："哇！又猜对了！你太棒啦！"

"Long ears, round face, furry body, and a short tail…" Diandian guessed, "Is it Little Rabbit?"
Little Rabbit said, "Wow! You're right again! You are awesome!"

小猫说："这儿有一位新朋友，你来猜猜他是谁？"

"又圆又硬，冰冰凉，这是什么呀？"胖熊点点说，
"小猫你真坏，拿铁桶来蒙我！"

Little Cat said, "We have got a new friend. Can you guess
who he is?"

"It's round, firm and freezing cold. What is it?" Diandian
said, "Little Cat, you are so bad. You are using an iron
bucket to trick me!"

小猫说：“哈哈！这回你猜不着了吧！这是机器人呀！”

Little Cat said, "Ha-ha! You don't know the answer this time, do you? It's a robot!"

胖熊点点急了：“下一个是谁？让我抱一抱，我肯定能猜对！来吧！”

Diandian was a little embarrassed. He wanted to give it another try. "Who's next? Let me hug you and I'll definitely figure out who you are! Come on!" said Diandian.

嗯……

Hummmm...

哎呀

哎呀

…… Ouch ouch...

"还从来没有人敢抱我呢！"小刺猬不好意思地说，"对不起，把你扎疼了吧？"

"No one ever dared to hug me before!" Little Porcupine was a little shy. He said, "I'm sorry! I must have poked you."

胖熊点点强忍住眼泪说：
"没关系,都怨我自己！不过,
不抱抱试试，哪能知道呢？"
大家都笑了。

Diandian tried hard to hold his tears and said, "It's OK. It was my own fault, but if I didn't hug you, I wouldn't have known it hurts this much." Everyone laughed.

绘本中的科学

—— 写给大人的话

触觉和视觉、听觉、嗅觉一样，是人体接收外界信号的重要方式。人体的触觉器官是皮肤，它包裹着整个体表，让我们可以随时感知外部世界：温度、湿度、软硬，以及不同物体的轮廓和材质等。不过，并不是每个部位的皮肤的触觉都同样灵敏，手指指腹的触觉是最敏感的，而小腿和背部是最迟钝的。当我们用两根相距0.5CM的钝针分别触压手指和背部的皮肤时，手指可以瞬间分辨出两根针，而背部皮肤却误认为只有一根针。

本书中出现了很多通过触觉可以感知到的概念：冷和热、软和硬、粗和细、长和短、光滑和粗糙……同时也告诉孩子们：被扎到、被烫到的话都会疼的，因此并不是所有东西都可随便碰哦。

疼呀！

Ouch!

软

硬

暖

冷

图书在版编目（CIP）数据

　疼呀痛啊：汉英对照 / 肖叶文；罗殷，焦天虹绘 . —— 北京：
连环画出版社，2017.4
　（聪明的伙伴）
　ISBN 978-7-5056-3312-4

　Ⅰ.①疼… Ⅱ.①肖… ②罗… ③焦… Ⅲ.①儿童故事 –
图画故事 – 中国 – 当代 Ⅳ.① I287.8

　中国版本图书馆 CIP 数据核字 (2016) 第 273107 号

聪明的伙伴·疼呀痛啊

文　　字：肖叶
绘　　画：罗殷 焦天虹
翻　　译：[美]斯蒂芬妮·陈

责任编辑：李滢　林晓阳　　　　　　版式设计：林晓阳
责任校对：马晓婷　　　　　　　　　责任印制：刘建春

出版发行：连环画出版社
地　　址：北京北总布胡同32号
邮　　编：100735
发行部电话：010-67517601
邮购部电话：010-67517797

制版印刷：北京尚唐印刷包装有限公司
装　　订：北京尚唐印刷包装有限公司

开　　本：889mm×1194mm　1/16　　印　　张：2.25
版　　次：2017年4月第1版　　　　　印　　次：2017年4月第1次印刷
书　　号：ISBN 978-7-5056-3312-4

定　　价：32.80元

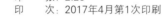

绿 色 印 刷　保 护 环 境　爱 护 健 康